RUFUS
and the
VERY SPECIAL BABY

By Carla Barnhill

Illustrated by Natasha Rimmington

First edition published 2016

Printed in United States

22 21 20 19 18 17 16   1 2 3 4 5 6 7 8

Book design by Tim Palin Creative

ISBN 9781506417622

Library of Congress Cataloging-in-Publication Data

Names: Barnhill, Carla, author. | Rimmington, Natasha, illustrator.
Title: Rufus and the very special baby: a Frolic Christmas story / written by Carla Barnhill; illustrated by Natasha Rimmington.
Description: First edition. | Minneapolis, MN: Sparkhouse Family, 2016. | Summary: Rufus wants to join his animal friends in visiting the newborn baby sent by God, but has no gift to bring. | Description based on print version record and CIP data provided by publisher; resource not viewed.
Identifiers: LCCN 2016021282 (print) | LCCN 2016006551 (ebook) | ISBN 9781506417769 (ebook) | ISBN 9781506417622 (hardcover: alk. paper)
Subjects: | CYAC: Gifts--Fiction. | Animals--Fiction. | Babies--Fiction. | Jesus Christ--Nativity--Fiction.
Classification: LCC PZ7.1.B3713 (print) | LCC PZ7.1.B3713 Ruf 2016 (ebook) | DDC [E]--dc23
LC record available at https://lccn.loc.gov/2016021282

VN0004589; 9781456417622; JUN2016

SPARK
HOUSE
FAMILY
sparkhouse.org

Rufus was getting ready for bed. He'd just curled up under his cape when suddenly, Ava came running.

"Get up, Rufus!" Ava shouted. "Something wonderful is happening!"

"Stop it, Ava. I'm sleeping," Rufus grumbled.

"But, Rufus, I have to tell you about the baby!"
Ava said.

Rufus's ears perked up.

"Just now, when I was in the field with the other sheep, angels filled the sky! They said that God sent a special baby boy as a gift to the whole world!"

Rufus leapt out of bed.
A special baby sent by God?

"Let's go find him!" Ava said. "The angels said
the baby would be in a manger. I'm going to
bring him some of my wool for a pillow.
You can bring a gift too!"

Wool is a good gift, thought Rufus.
I wonder what I could give a baby.

A nice bone? A smelly fish? A ball of string?

No, those were gifts for a baby dog,
not a baby person.

Rufus thought and thought. Then he came to a conclusion. *I don't have anything special enough to give to a baby from God.*

But Rufus wanted to see the baby. Maybe he could just take a peek. So he followed after Ava.

Ava and Rufus walked down the path and found Jo. Ava told him about the special baby.

"I want to give something to the baby too," said Jo. He grabbed a big armful of hay.

"This hay will make a comfy bed for the new baby," he told Ava.

That's a good gift, thought Rufus. *The baby will like having a soft place to sleep.*

Rufus, Ava, and Jo kept walking. Soon they found Hal. Ava told him all about the baby.

"I want to bring the baby something that will make him smile," said Hal.

Hal looked at the beautiful flowers in the field.

"This is the biggest, brightest flower in the whole field," Hal said. "It will make the baby smile."

That's a good gift, Rufus thought. *The baby will like having something nice to look at.*

Soon the friends found Uri. Ava told her all about the baby.

"We're all bringing gifts for the baby," Ava said. "Maybe you can sing him a lullaby!"

Uri cooed and nodded.

Ava, Jo, Hal, and Uri headed toward
the stable to find the baby.

But Rufus hung his head and kicked sadly at the ground. *Everyone has a gift but me*, he thought.

If only I had something special to give the baby too.

Ava, Jo, Hal, and Uri walked into a small building filled with shining light.

Rufus peeked through the door.
And then he saw the baby.

A woman rocked him in her arms.
A man was cleaning out a wooden manger
that usually held food for the cows.

The baby fussed and cried.

Ava, Jo, Hal, and Uri tiptoed up to the family.

Jo put his bundle of hay into the manger. Ava added her wool to make a pillow for the baby's head.

The mother laid the baby on the wool and the hay. Right away, the baby stopped crying. He snuggled into the bed that Ava and Jo had made for him.

Next, Hal scurried up to the manger and set his flower gently inside. The baby's eyes seemed to shine with delight.

Uri flew up into the rafters and sang a
beautiful song. The baby listened for a while,
then closed his eyes and let out a sigh.

Rufus watched from the edge of the room. Everyone had found just the right gift to welcome this special baby. But Rufus didn't have anything to give. His tail drooped. He began shuffling out the door.

But when Rufus heard Ava whispering to the others, he stopped.

"The baby's mother said his name is Jesus," said Ava. "She said he's a sign of God's love for the whole world."

Rufus looked again at the manger. And then he saw something he hadn't noticed before.

The baby wasn't sleeping. He was shivering. Cold air was blowing from the door and keeping him awake.

Suddenly, Rufus knew exactly
what his gift should be.

It wasn't going to be easy. Could he give away
his very favorite something? Rufus needed help.

Dear God, you gave the special gift of Jesus to the whole world. Please help me give away something I love to someone who needs it more than me. Amen.

Rufus took a deep breath and walked up to
the manger.

He untied his cape and gently laid it on the baby.
Jesus blinked his big brown eyes at Rufus, then
cooed and fell asleep under the warm red cape.

As the friends started for home, Ava and the others walked up to Rufus.

"I can't believe you gave him your cape," Ava whispered.

"I wanted to give him something special," said Rufus, "because he's a special baby, isn't he?"

"He is, Rufus," said Ava.

And together, they turned to gaze at this very special baby—this very special gift.

ABOUT THE STORY

The Frolic friends are excited to meet a very special baby and share their gifts to welcome him. But Rufus isn't so sure. A prayer about giving helps him find just the right way to celebrate this surprising gift from God.

DELIGHT IN READING TOGETHER

Together, talk about times you've received a special gift. How did you feel? Questions like this can help children connect their experiences to the story in meaningful ways.

DEVELOPMENT CONNECTION

As you prepare Christmas gifts for family and friends, talk to your child about the reasons we give presents at Christmas. Talk about how good it feels to give to those we love and those in need.

FAITH CONNECTION

The story of the first Christmas is the story of God's unending love for us. Our great God wants nothing less than to walk with us, talk with us, and be in a relationship with us. The gifts we give one another at Christmas remind us of the goodness of the very first Christmas night and the glorious gift of God's love.

The Word became flesh and made his dwelling among us.

    John 1:14

SAY A PRAYER

Share this prayer Rufus said when he needed help giving his gift:

Dear God, you gave the special gift of Jesus to the whole world. Please help me give away something I love to someone who needs it more than me.

Amen.